# DREAM HOUSE

## A SHORT STORY

## ALEXANDRIA BLAELOCK

BlueMere Books
MELBOURNE, AUSTRALIA

For permission requests, please contact
enquiries@bluemerebooks.com.

Ordering Information:
Discounts are available on quantity purchases. For details, contact orders@bluemerebooks.com.

Dream House/Alexandria Blaelock
paperback ISBN: 978-1-922744-38-8
digital ISBN: 978-1-922744-39-5

# DREAM HOUSE

Bill kicked the stand of his red postie motorcycle out, and let the bike lean on the rest.

He took his helmet and gloves off, putting the gloves in the helmet and placing it in the mailbag attached to the handlebars before scratching his head and ruffling his hair with both hands to help the sweat evaporate.

And paused for a moment to enjoy the stillness in his body.

Without removing his sunglasses, turned his face towards the sun, closed his eyes and took a deep breath of the fresh gum scented air.

Then he stood and lifted his leg over the bike and placing his hands on the small of his back, leaned back, folding his shoulders out to stretch out his chest.

That was a bit better.

Intertwining his arms and pushing them out, he leaned forward to stretch his back and shoulders. Then rocked his head from side to side stretching out his neck as he ripped open his jacket and flapped it to get a breeze through his sweaty shirt.

Having eased his tense body, he pulled a stainless steel water flask from the bike's saddlebag, and took a swig, swishing it around his dry mouth before swallowing.

The water always tasted better when he hit the old part of the suburb.

And one day, when he could afford it, he wanted to buy a house around here.

And if he could have his pick, it would be old Mrs Pearson's - number 17 Mason Close.

A beautiful, old, Federation style, white weatherboard cottage with a heritage red steel roof, on a big block halfway up a hill in a quiet cul-de-sac.

With highly scented yellow David Austin roses in the front garden and gum trees in the back.

Bluestone gravel driveway and white picket fence.

Throw in the wicker porch setting, and you've got yourself a deal.

He signed and leaned on the green mail distribution box, taking another drink from his flask.

The gum tree the box was under didn't cast much shade, but the smell of it made this the best place to take a moment to rest on his entire delivery run.

Plus, magpies roosted in it, and he loved listening to their melodic conversations.

A young-un settled in a branch close by and looked at him intently. He pulled a small snack from his pocket, and the bird snatched it from his hand and flew higher up into the tree.

Bill knew he shouldn't feed the thing, but there was swooping season to think about.

While his neck drape protected him from the sun and rain, it wasn't so useful when swooping season came around.

The magpies had chased off the postie before him, and he wanted to stay on their good side!

Running a little behind, he checked the time and put his water bottle away.

Then unlocked the distribution box, took out the pre-sorted mail and quickly sorted some into the front bag, and the rest into the saddlebags. Resealed the Velcro on his jacket, gloves and helmet, and he was ready to go again.

The first section of Tuesday's delivery run was uneventful. While email slowed down the letters, it meant more small packages, but that day, there wasn't much to deliver.

Perhaps that's why the bike's brakes still squeaked annoyingly every time he slowed.

Not enough money to fix them properly, or maintain spares, or whatever.

Maybe he was 16th in the queue, just like the library waiting list for the latest Grisham novel.

Fortunately, nothing for 10 Grant Street, so the terrier had to content itself with running along the fence, barking like he was demon-possessed as the bike sped past.

Tempting as it was, he did not make a face or raise any fingers in the dog's direction.

Nearly wiped out by a delivery van reversing out of 52 Moore Street without looking. Or tooting their horn.

Though to be fair, delivery drivers had their own issues to deal with.

Then nearly run off the road by a car coming round the roundabout at the other end. Not looking, not giving way, too busy thinking they were too important to consider the needs of any other road users.

Just like all the others.

Though it did make delivering mail a more exciting career than it might otherwise seem.

Had to slow down and weave in and out of badly placed rubbish bins in Clementine Avenue. Honestly, it's not like Council didn't have guidelines about that. Hopefully, the ones recommended by the Postal Corporation.

Almost drove into an enormous pothole on Erica Avenue. It'd been there for weeks, so you'd think by now he'd have habituated the out-swing to avoid it.

He wondered how much longer before they fixed it. Maybe they were going to wait until the current round of road works were complete so they could dig it all up again.

Around the corner into Bridge Road and collided with a pile of prunings haphazardly stacked up waiting for collection. It might be hot, but thank goodness for the heavy-duty protective gear.

Bill quietly but firmly cursed as he hauled himself upright and dragged the bike back out of the mess.

Kicking what was left of the stack for good measure and leaving it for the resident to sort out.

He walked the bike the length of one house and garden to make sure it was fine to keep riding, before propping it up and walking back to take a couple of photos of the mess. He tapped out an Incident Notification Form on his postie phone, attached the pictures and sent them into Head Office.

The stack was probably a bit high for the guys who'd be coming out to take the prunings away anyway. He'd probably done them a favour collapsing it down a bit.

A package to deliver at 75 Spencer Street, so he propped the bike and walked to the door. Rang the doorbell, and after a beat or two, knocked on the door as well. No answer.

Double checked the address to make sure it was the right house, then left it by the door, trying to make sure it wasn't visible from the street.

Took a photo and sent it back to Head Office as proof of delivery.

Paused to scratch the head of a calico cat sunning itself on the porch on the way back to his bike.

All in all, just another day delivering the mail.

Rain, hail or shine.

Or as the Corporation expressed it, "committed to providing trusted, relevant and reliable services."

Load of Marketing BS if you asked him.

And if you asked, he'd have to be honest and say that as usual, he was trying to make up a bit of time so he could slow down and enjoy the ride along Mason Close.

He paused at the bottom of the street and looked up the tree-lined road to the top of the hill.

Something about all those trees, clustered in small arboreal communities, as if they were slowly migrating downhill was relaxing.

Maybe the Japanese were onto something with the whole forest bathing thing.

It was certainly way more restful than looking along his street at all the tower apartment buildings.

More sun and air for one thing.

More green for another.

Less graffiti, less rubbish and less of a youth "problem."

He cruised slowly up the street, slowing here and there to lean the bike and stuff letters in mailboxes.

Or behind the fence and on top of the box.

That wasn't really fair, there was no gang culture where he lived.

It was just a bunch of kids with nothing better to do. Sooner he got his out of there, the better.

He put number 32's mail back in the bag because they still hadn't replaced their mailbox.

He'd tucked a notice in the door a week ago telling them the mail would be stored at the local post office for seven days before being returned to sender until a new box was installed.

The place looked a bit unkempt, and he wondered if anyone still lived there.

Reaching the top of Mason Close, he paused and looked back down. From this angle, steep enough to be slightly vertiginous.

During school holidays, the space was crowded with kids who plodded up the hill pushing bicycles or carrying skateboards so they could coast back down.

And it was something he knew his kids would love to do as well.

Hell, some days, he enjoyed the coast down too.

Always slowing down to take in the full glory of number 17.

It was amazing how the view changed so much from day to day.

Today, there seemed to be a pile of filthy old clothing abandoned in the front garden.

Bill was a couple of houses down when it occurred to him that perhaps the pile of old clothes was actually Mrs Pearson, who was becoming increasingly frail.

It wasn't any of his business, but she was a charming lady, always ready to a chat if she was in the garden when he dropped the mail off.

And always offered him a cold drink when he delivered a package.

He couldn't just drive on without checking.

It was going to be a scorching hot day, and if she'd fallen, and couldn't get up, she might not last the day.

He turned back.

It was Mrs Pearson. Face down on the front lawn

Bill scanned the area and saw no obvious hazards so he got off the bike and headed toward her.

"Mrs Pearson, are you all right?" he asked.

She didn't move, or say anything.

"Mrs Pearson?" he asked, kneeling beside her and giving her shoulder a little shake.

Still no response.

He ripped his gloves off and gently rolled her on her back, tilting her head back and lifting her chin.

Bill turned his head and listened for breathing while he watched her chest and saw the faintest sign of movement.

Thank goodness.

A quick check of her clothes found no blood, and while her arms and legs were that peculiar, papery bluey white that elderly people's skin is prone to be, didn't seem to be cut or bitten.

Bill exhaled in a relieved whoosh.

He bent her closest arm upwards at the elbow, making sure her palm was facing up, then brought her other arm across her chest, resting the back of her hand against her cheek.

He found the leg furthest from him, and pulled it up through a fistful of skirts, so her foot was flat on the ground, then holding her knee and the hand on her cheek, rolled her body towards him, easing her into the recovery position.

Then tilted her head so her airway stayed open, propping it up with the hand on her cheek while he called for an ambulance.

Every five minutes or so, he called her name to see if she was responsive, then put his head close to hers to check she was still breathing.

Bill was about to roll her onto her other side when the ambulance finally arrived, and he could step back to let the ambos take over.

As they prepared to take her away, he gave them his contact number, just in case.

And as he watched them drive away, hoped she was going to be okay.

He filled out another incident form and sent it to Head Office.

He had no idea whether Mrs Pearson had family nearby or not, but he wrote a note on a Failure to Deliver Card and left it in the mailbox.

Just in case.

The rest of his run passed in a daze and the first thing he did when he got home was open a beer and sit out on the tiny balcony of his flat to drink it.

And a couple more after that.

It was such awful bad luck.

When he checked the next day, his note was still there. And the day after that, and the day after that. And the same the following Monday too. So, he stopped checking.

«« • »»

A few weeks later, she was sitting on the porch, and he had the idea she was waiting for him.

He rode up the drive and got off the bike to talk to her.

"Lemonade?" She offered, "homemade?"

"I shouldn't, but yes. Thank you."

She filled a glass with the bitter, slightly sweet, pale yellow liquid.

"It seems I should thank you. I'm told, if not for you, I would have died."

He nodded his head, just once.

She sighed. "At my age, living is not always the best option."

"I'm sorry."

"Not your fault lad," she patted his leg, "it's just the nature of life.

But I have no family, so now I have to sell the house and move into a nursing home to get "proper" care."

"I'll buy it," he blurted.

"I beg your pardon?"

"I'm sorry. I suppose you'd call me forward. But I love your house, and, well, I'll buy it."

The old woman smiled a little, "yes, I suppose I would call you forward. But why do you want to buy the house?"

"Because it's beautiful."

"It is that on the outside, but I'm an old woman, it might be different on the inside."

"I imagine it might be a bit old-fashioned on the inside, and maybe a bit worn down and a bit behind on the maintenance, but anyone who looks as neat and elegant as you, and takes such good care of their garden is probably not going to let things slide in the house."

"Things have run down a little since my Bill died, but I do my best."

"Was that your husband's name? Bill."

"Yes, William Garrett Pearson. He had a heart attack and died a few years ago."

Bill snorted, "that's funny, my name is William Grant Peterson."

She smiled, "that is rather curious. Would you like to see the inside?"

"I would love to."

Mrs Pearson leveraged herself out of her chair with a walking stick topped with a crystal knob and opened the screen door for him.

He stepped inside and waited for her.

She poked him with the walking stick, "don't wait for me boy, go have a look round."

"Yes, Miss Havisham," the words were out of his mouth before he could stop them.

Fortunately, she snorted and tapped the stick on the ground.

"Miss Havisham indeed. I'll wait outside," she said, letting the door swing closed in his face as she turned back to her seat.

Bill walked from room to room in awe.

Even though the last time it had been updated was clearly the fifties, the interior was immaculate.

His mother's home had been stuffed full of junk when she passed away, with next to nothing salvageable let alone saleable.

He and his sister had filled three of the big skips with rubbish, and by the time they'd paid for all that, there was just enough money left in the estate to go out for dinner.

By contrast, Mrs Pearson's home was austere. Each room held a simple suite of furniture, and one significant piece of art, whether canvas, sculpture or ceramic.

Three bedrooms and one bathroom might be considered small by most, but the ceilings were high and the rooms a good size, especially with so little furniture.

And with the curtains closed over the slightly ajar double-hung windows, the rooms were dim and cool, so the lack of air conditioning might not be a problem.

Unlike his tiny flat, exposed to the sun throughout the Summer.

Out the back, a verandah ran the full length of the house, shading it from the sun, and providing a comfortable vantage point to enjoy the garden, a sort of natural native landscape.

There was plenty of room to move.

To breath.

To take up space.

He had no trouble imagining his family eating in the dining room, queueing up for the toilet, and having barbecues on the verandah.

Bill wanted the house more than he'd wanted his wife.

And he'd wanted her a lot.

But he had to be fair to Mrs Pearson.

He had to pay her market price, and he wasn't entirely sure he could afford that.

"Well?" she asked when he returned to the front porch.

He opened his mouth, but no words came out, so he shrugged his shoulders.

She smiled, "I know. I felt the same when I first saw her too."

"Her?"

"Her. The garden was full of Marguerite Daisies that day, so we started calling the house Marguerite."

"Suits her."

"Indeed," she said, leaning back in her chair, "we bought her not long after we married. I'll miss her, but she's not the same without him."

She wiped a tear from her eye.

"Right. I'll get three market appraisals, and we can talk some more when we see what they come back as. Deal?"

"Deal," he said.

She spat in her hand and held it out for him to shake. He looked at it for a moment, then spat in his own and clasped hers in both of his.

He hadn't made a commitment to do more than talk about it further, but he hoped his wife would forgive him.

Several weeks later, he saw Mrs Pearson on the porch, waiting for him.

He pulled in, walked her mail up to her, and accepted her invitation to sit and take some lemonade.

He sat on the edge of the chair.

"Your wife's a lovely young thing, isn't she?"

"When did you meet Sandra?"

"She popped out to say hello, and take a look at the house a week or two ago."

"She didn't tell me that!"

"Why would she Bill?"

"Well... Um... Ah..."

Mrs Pearson sipped some lemonade, "she loved the house, you know."

Bill relaxed a little, and gulped half his glass.

"Let's move on," she handed him some folded pages, "here are the quotes."

He flicked through the pages, outrage warring with relief."

"Surely this is not enough for the property."

"Apparently everyone's looking for four bedrooms and at least two bathrooms these days. All the agents I spoke to said I'd be lucky if I even got land value because the house would probably be knocked down by the new owner."

"Sacrilege!"

"I know, but there you have it."

"I promise I won't knock Marguerite down."

"I think she knows it too.

"Now. What say we go with the highest quote and I'll throw in the furniture and most of the other bits and pieces."

"That's not enough Mrs Pearson, and what will you use yourself?"

She grimaced as she nodded at the house, "I have to make do with their cheap and nasty furniture, and they're quite prescriptive about what I can take, which is next to nothing."

"Well, yes, but—"

"And quite simply, I can't be bothered making any arrangements to get rid of it all."

"Oh. Ah. Okay then."

She handed him another set of papers, "I bought a sales contract from the newsagent, and I've filled all the bits in. Why don't you take it home to Sandra, and pop back tomorrow to let me know what you're going to do."

《《　•　》》

It seemed like no time at all before the bright sunny morning of moving day arrived. The loan had gone through without a hitch, the deposit paid, bags and boxes packed and on the truck.

The family piled in the car, with a big bunch of flowers and some homemade ANZAC cookies for Mrs Pearson.

She greeted them with kisses and held the door open for the kids to run through, shrieking at each other, and out the back to the verandah before running back in shouting about a picnic.

Mrs Pearson left her small suitcase by the door and took them out to the verandah and the little picnic she'd set up.

Champagne on ice for the adults, and fizzy drinks for the kids.

A Victoria sponge, cucumber sandwiches, fresh strawberries with sweetened cream and potato chips.

She poured drinks for the kids, then the Champagne for the adults. Holding her glass up as a toast, she said, "I hope you'll be as happy here as Bill and I were."

"And we hope you'll be happy too," Bill replied.

Mrs Pearson snorted, but said, "cheers" and sipped the wine.

The doorbell rang.

"That'll be your movers," she said, "you go sort it out, and I'll watch the kids."

"They're a bit of a handful, are you sure you'll be okay?"

Mrs Pearson gestured at them halfway up a tree, "I'm pretty sure they'll be fine a while longer."

Bill nodded and went back into the house.

"Thanks so much," Sandra said, and chased after him.

It took nearly an hour for the movers to unpack the truck and stack all their belongings in the dining room and leave.

Bill and Sandra went back out the back and saw Mrs Pearson had slumped a little in her chair, her chin resting on her chest.

He made a step towards her, but Sandra put out a hand to stop her.

"Leave her. She's fallen asleep, let her rest a little longer. It's going to be hard for her to leave the house she spent her entire married life in."

Bill patted his wife's hand and smiled down at her. "I hope our marriage is as long and happy as hers."

She wrinkled her nose as she smiled back, "me too."

They left her a little longer while they worked in the kitchen together to make a thick, spicy vegetable soup for lunch to go with the fresh-baked bread rolls they'd bought on the way.

Mrs Pearson was a little embarrassed to be woken but enjoyed her lunch.

Bill and Sandra took the kids for a walk around the neighbourhood to give Mrs Pearson a chance to say goodbye to her home, and when they got back, she'd gone.

Bill felt the house was sad to see her go, so he patted the hallway door frame as he passed through into the kitchen, "Don't worry Marguerite," he told it, "we're here for you."

His wife and children laughed at him, but they all patted the hallway door frame on their way through too.

That evening, after the kids had gone to bed, Bill and Sandra sat together on a bench on the back verandah, holding hands and enjoying the sunset.

"Do you think houses have souls?" he asked his wife.

"Of course," she replied, "and I think owners leave a little piece of theirs behind when they go."

"Mmmm," said Bill, "I think this is a happy house."

She squeezed his hand, "Yes. We're very lucky. This is a house people keep for a long time."

"I'm so glad to get out of that flat."

"We'll be happier here, I'm sure."
He squeezed her hand, "I know we will."


**THE END**

# ABOUT THE AUTHOR

Alexandria Blaelock writes stories, some of them for *Ellery Queen's Mystery Magazine* and *Pulphouse Fiction Magazine*. She's also written four self-help books applying business techniques to personal matters like getting dressed, cleaning house, and feeding your friends.

As a recovering Project Manager, she's probably too fond of sticking to plan. She lives in a forest because she enjoys birdsong, the scent of gum leaves and the sun on her face. When not telecommuting to parallel universes from her Melbourne based imagination, she watches K-dramas, talks to animals, and drinks Campari.
At the same time.

Discover more at www.alexandriablaelock.com.

# BOOKS BY ALEXANDRIA BLAELOCK

## SHORT STORY COLLECTIONS

The Histories of Hayward Hall
Lovelorn, Lovestruck and Love at First Sight
Common or Garden Variety Heroes
Case Files of the Wilkinson Detective Agency
Unavoidable Fates
Christmas Travesties
Five Faces of Felicia Clarke

## OTHER FICTION

That Love Nonsense

## MS BLAELOCK'S BOOKS

Stress Free Dinner Parties
Signature Wardrobe Planning
Holistic Personal Finance
Minimally Viable Housekeeping
Planning a Life Worth Living

# SELECTED SHORT STORIES

Alma's Grace
Balancing the Book
Carmelita Basingstoke
Fate in Your Hands
Kiss of Death
Lady of the Looking Glass
Life in the Security Directorate
Long Weekend in the Snow
Love in the Past Tense
Love in the Security Directorate
Morning Star, Evening Star, Superstar
Needy Bitch
Payton's Run
Phoenix Child
Secret Singer
Shining Star
Ship in a Bottle
Simone Says Hands in the Air
Special Relativity in Space
The Bygone Boyfriend
The Day the Schedule Broke
The Ghost Detectors
The Guardian's Vigil
The Mince Pie Mystery
The Mystery of the Master Suite
The Pseudonym's Bride
The Shadow Thieves
The Space-Time Paradox
Toy Soldiers